CW01218754

Presidents' Day

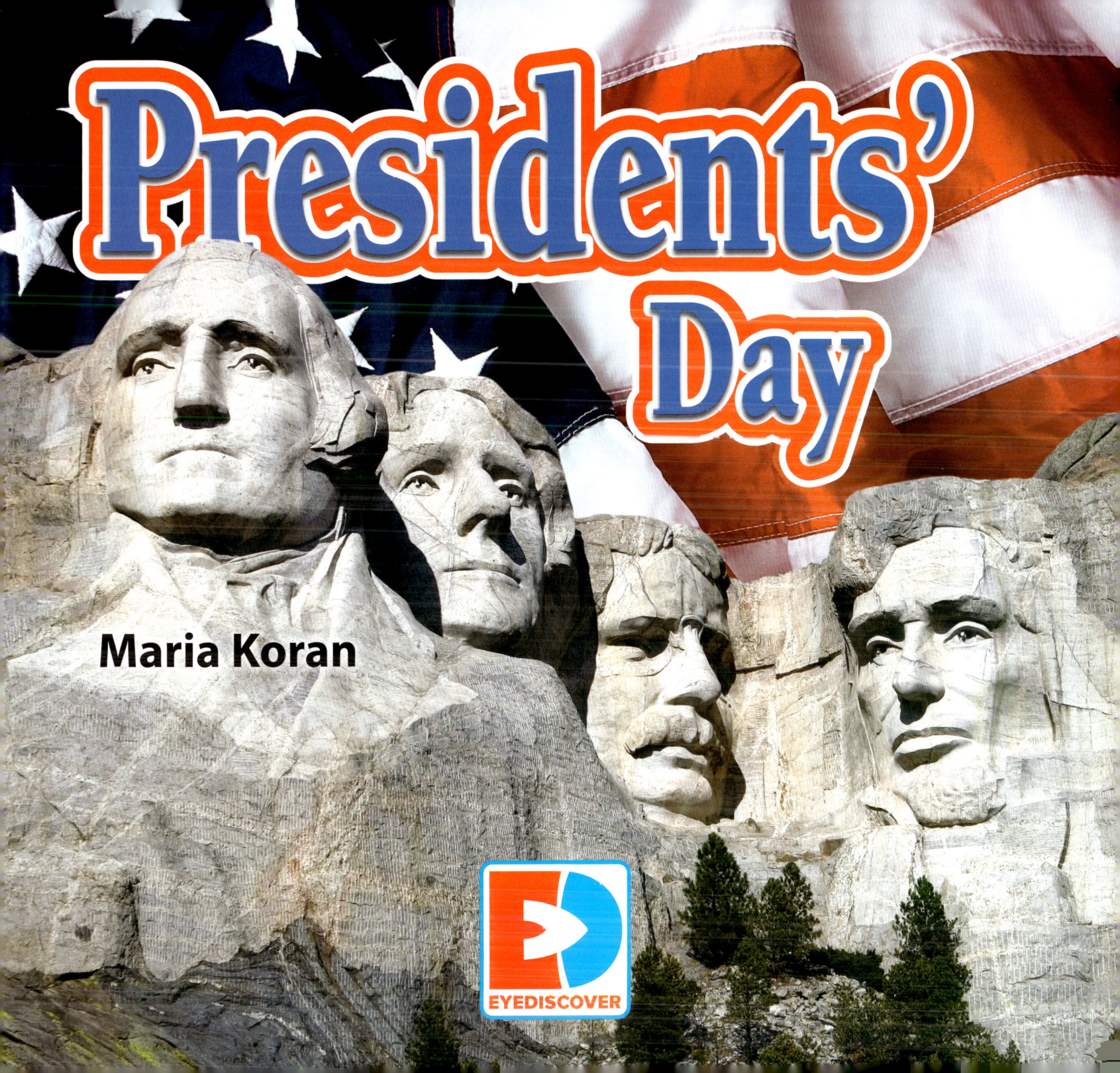

Maria Koran

EYEDISCOVER

Go to **www.eyediscover.com** and enter this book's unique code.

BOOK CODE

AVM66967

EYEDISCOVER brings you optic readalongs that support active learning.

Published by AV² by Weigl
350 5th Avenue, 59th Floor New York, NY 10118
Website: www.eyediscover.com

Copyright ©2020 AV² by Weigl
All rights reserved. No part of this publication may be reproduced, stored in a retrieval system, or transmitted in any form or by any means, electronic, mechanical, photocopying, recording, or otherwise, without the prior written permission of the publisher.

Library of Congress Control Number: 2019945847

ISBN 978-1-7911-0816-8 (hardcover)

Printed in Guangzhou, China
1 2 3 4 5 6 7 8 9 0 23 22 21 20 19

072019
121818

Project Coordinator: John Willis
Designers: Mandy Christiansen and Ana María Vidal

Weigl acknowledges Alamy, Getty Images, and iStock as the primary image suppliers for this title.

EYEDISCOVER provides enriched content, optimized for tablet use, that supplements and complements this book. EYEDISCOVER books strive to create inspired learning and engage young minds in a total learning experience.

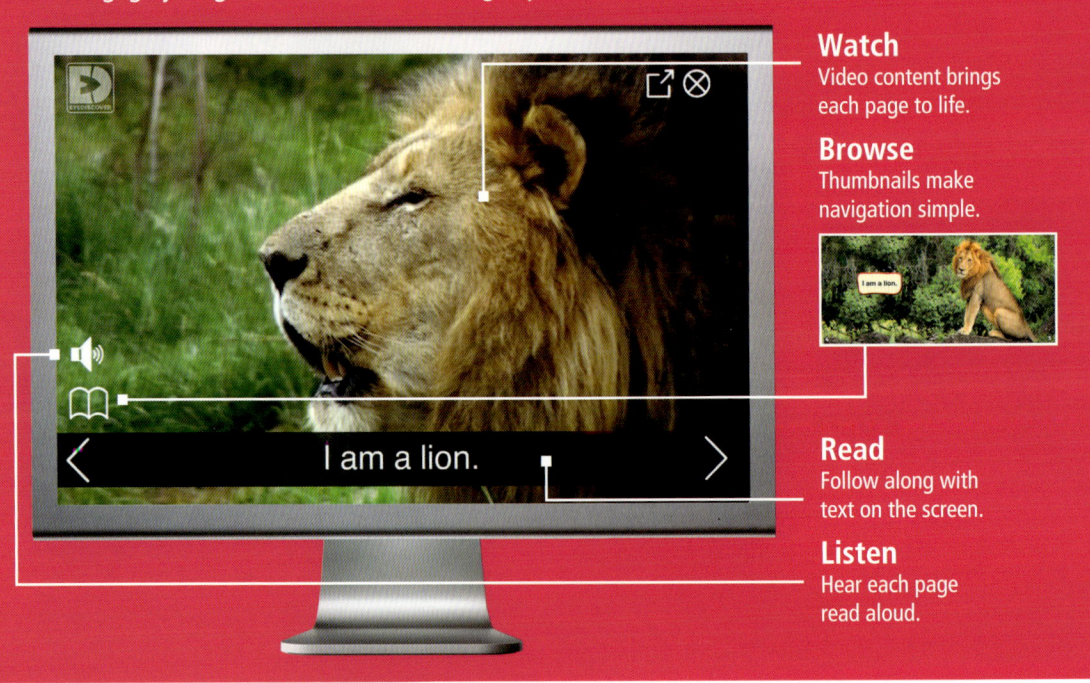

Watch
Video content brings each page to life.

Browse
Thumbnails make navigation simple.

Read
Follow along with text on the screen.

Listen
Hear each page read aloud.

Your EYEDISCOVER Optic Readalongs come alive with...

Audio
Listen to the entire book read aloud.

Video
High resolution videos turn each spread into an optic readalong.

OPTIMIZED FOR
- ✓ TABLETS
- ✓ WHITEBOARDS
- ✓ COMPUTERS
- ✓ AND MUCH MORE!

Presidents' Day

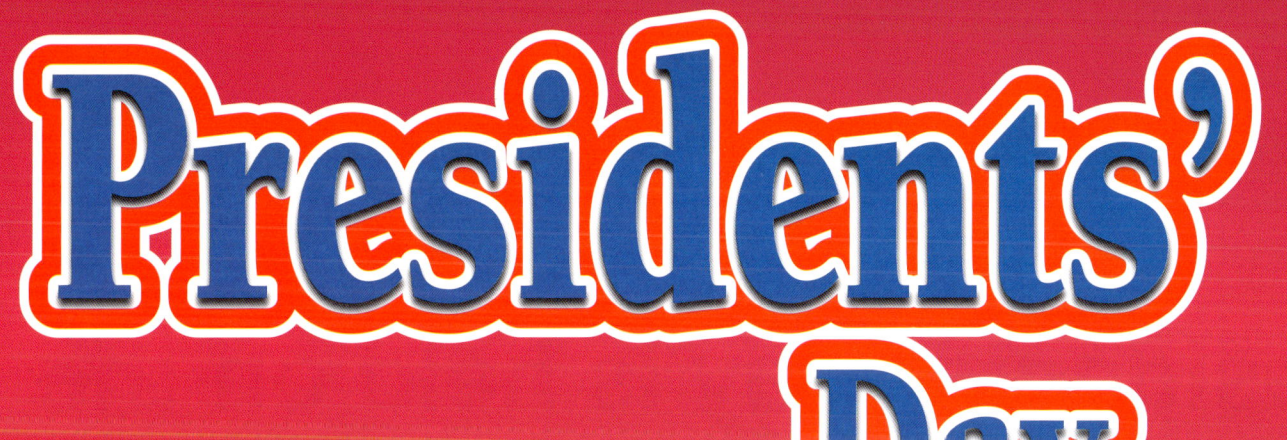

In this book, you will learn about

- what it is
- why we celebrate it
- how we celebrate it

and much more!

Presidents' Day is held on the third Monday of each February. It started as a way to honor President George Washington.

5

6

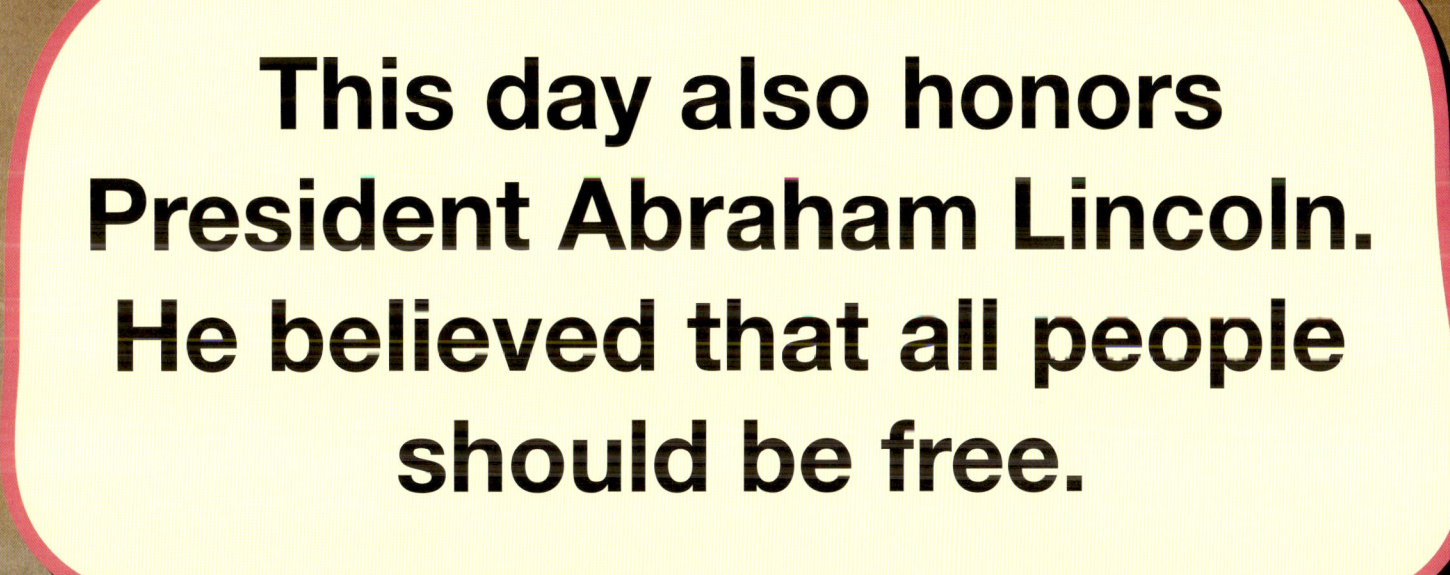

This day also honors President Abraham Lincoln. He believed that all people should be free.

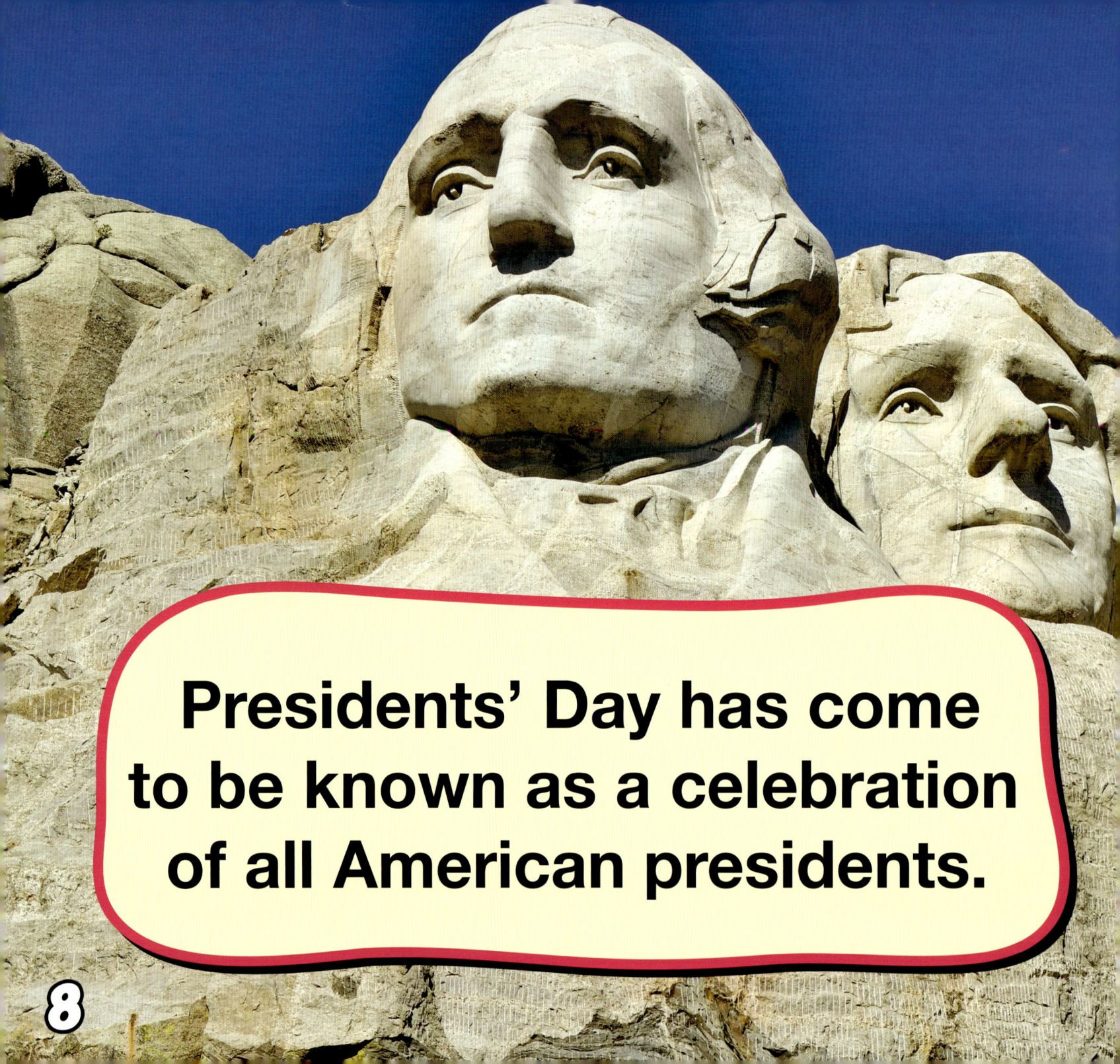

Presidents' Day has come to be known as a celebration of all American presidents.

9

10

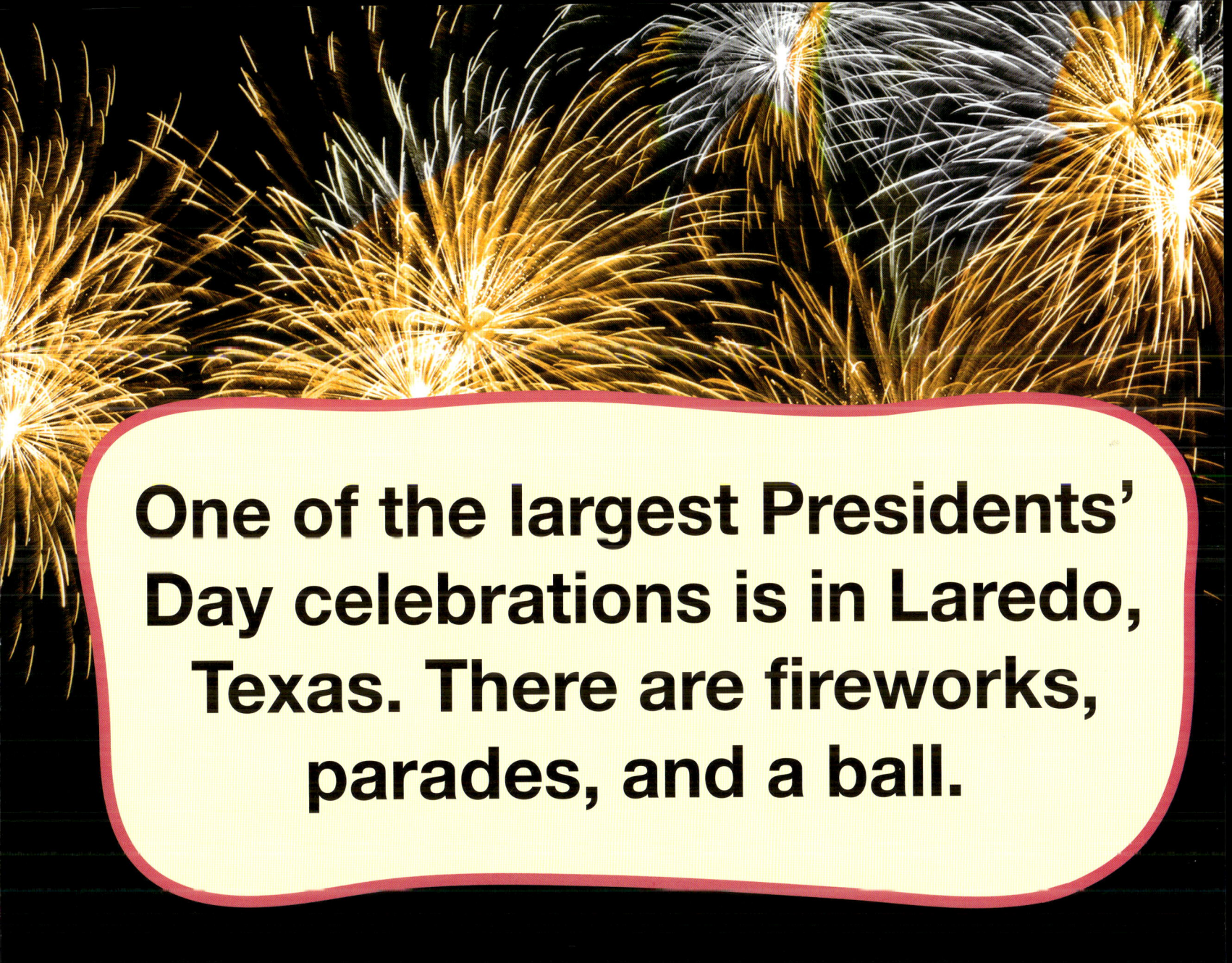

One of the largest Presidents' Day celebrations is in Laredo, Texas. There are fireworks, parades, and a ball.

12

Presidents' Day parade floats are often covered in red, white, and blue. These are the colors of the American flag.

Some people dress up on Presidents' Day. They act out events from the past.

15

IS ENSHRINED FOREVER

Many people visit monuments on Presidents' Day. They lay wreaths to honor past presidents.

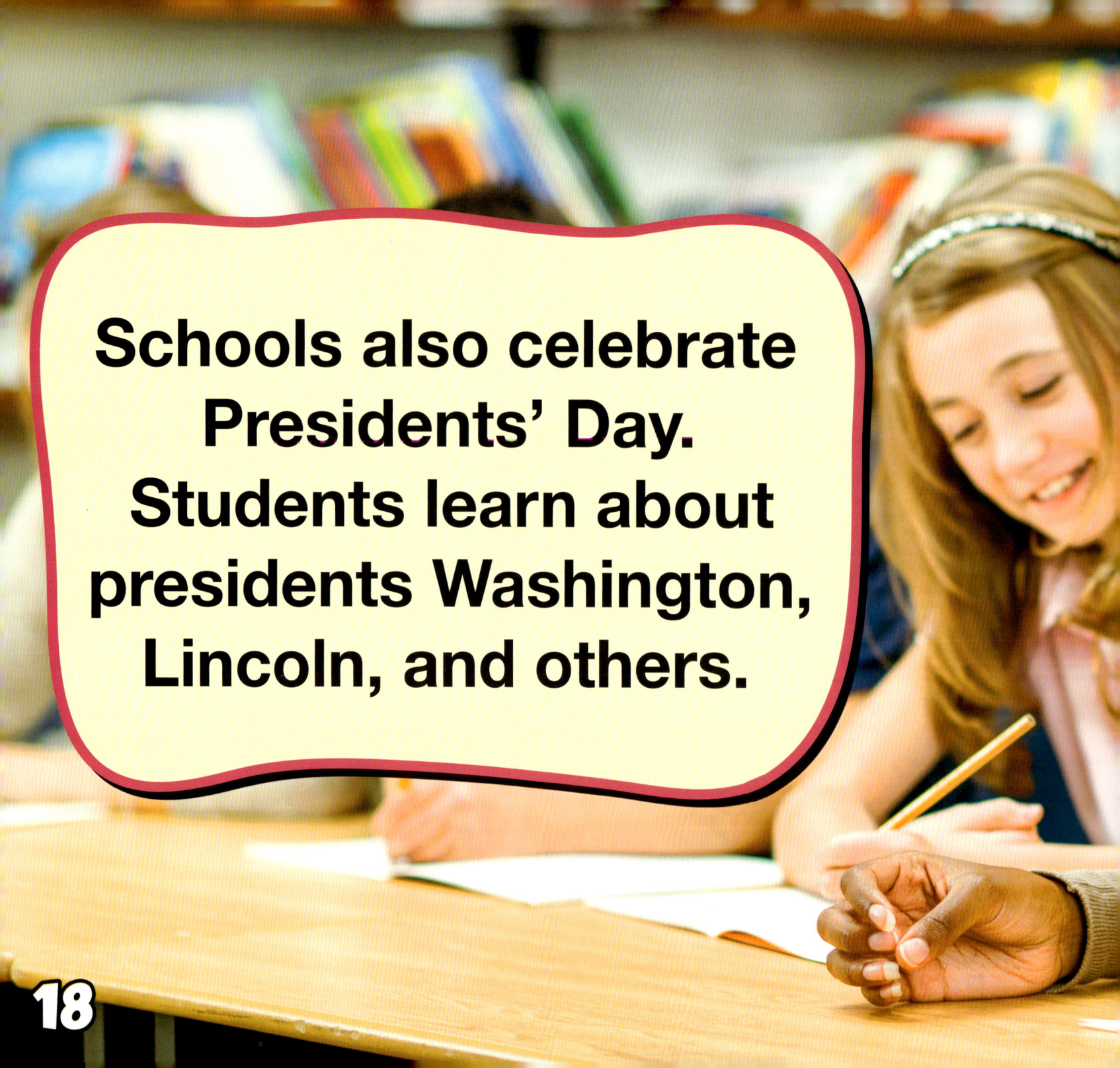

Schools also celebrate Presidents' Day. Students learn about presidents Washington, Lincoln, and others.

19

Presidents' Day is a time to bring the past to life.

21

PRESIDENTS' DAY FACTS

George Washington's birthday first became a holiday more than **120** years ago.

Four U.S. presidents were **born in February.** They are George Washington, Abraham Lincoln, William Harrison, and Ronald Reagan.

Presidents' Day was **moved** to a Monday in 1968.

Presidents' Day is **officially** called **Washington's Birthday**.

George Washington was the **first** U.S. president.

23

KEY WORDS

Research has shown that as much as 65 percent of all written material published in English is made up of 300 words. These 300 words cannot be taught using pictures or learned by sounding them out. They must be recognized by sight. This book contains 43 common sight words to help young readers improve their reading fluency and comprehension. This book also teaches young readers several important content words, such as proper nouns. These words are paired with pictures to aid in learning and improve understanding.

Page	Sight Words First Appearance
4	a, as, day, each, is, it, of, on, started, the, to, way
7	all, also, be, he, people, should, that, this
8	American, come, has
11	are, and, in, one, there
13	often, these, white
14	from, out, some, they, up
17	many
18	about, learn, others, schools
20	life, time

Page	Content Words First Appearance
4	February, George Washington, Monday, Presidents' Day
7	Abraham Lincoln
8	celebration
11	ball, fireworks, Laredo, parades, Texas
13	flag, floats
14	events
17	monuments, wreaths
18	students

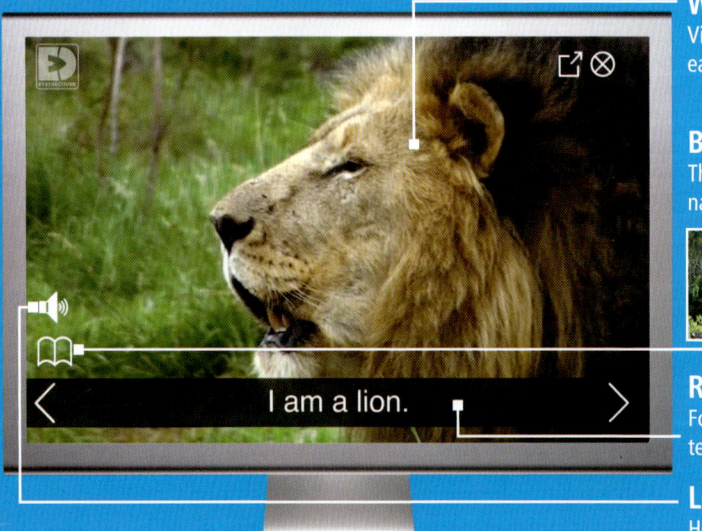

Watch Video content brings each page to life.

Browse Thumbnails make navigation simple.

Read Follow along with text on the screen.

Listen Hear each page read aloud.

Go to www.eyediscover.com and enter this book's unique code.

BOOK CODE

AVM66967